Stork's Landing

To my granddaughter Ella. Storks may not bring babies, but you arrived just in time
for this book. May we have many happy story hours together.—T. L.W.

For Dale and Yana—A.S.

KAR-BEN PUBLISHING
A division of Lerner Publishing Group, Inc.
241 First Avenue North
Minneapolis, MN 55401 USA
1-800-4-KARBEN

Website address: www.karben.com

Main body text set in Edwardian Medium Std 15/22. Typeface provided by International Typeface Corp.

Library of Congress Cataloging-in-Publication Data

Lehman-Wilzig, Tami.
     Stork's landing / by Tami Lehman-Wilzig ; illustrated by Anna Shuttlewood.
        pages   cm.
     ISBN 978-1-4677-1395-5 (lib. bdg. : alk. paper)
     ISBN 978-1-4677-4673-1 (eBook)
     1. Storks—Fiction. 2. Wildlife rescue—Fiction. 3. Birds—Migration—Fiction.
   4. Israel—Fiction.] I. Shuttlewood, Anna, illustrator. II. Title.
     PZ7.L53223St 2014
     [E]—dc23   2013021756

PJ Library Edition ISBN 978-1-4677-1397-9

Manufactured in China
2-1009812-13447-7/25/2023

0424/B449/A6

Stork's Landing

Tami Lehman-Wilzig

illustrated by Anna Shuttlewood

KAR-BEN
PUBLISHING

Maya hears the sound of flapping wings. It's spring on the kibbutz. A large flock of white storks flies overhead, making its way from Africa to Europe, where they will spend the summer. Maya knows the storks will land on the kibbutz to rest. They always do.

Maya starts running. She hopes that Abba and the other fish farmers have covered the ponds with nets to protect the fish.

One of the storks circles, looking hungrily for her next meal.

As the bird tries to land, her long, graceful legs get caught in the net. She tries to set herself free, but can't. Scared, she flaps her wings until c-r-a-c-k, one wing breaks. Sad and hurt, the stork lowers her head just as Maya reaches the pond.

Maya takes out her walkie-talkie. "S-O-S. Stork in net," she radios her father.

"I'm on my way," he signals back.

When Abba arrives, he gently lifts the injured stork.

"Looks like the vet will have to operate."

But the broken wing cannot be fixed.

"We have to take care of her," Maya insists.
"She is so beautiful, and now she can't move."

The fish farmers build the stork a nest surrounded by a
protective tire. Maya visits her every day. She names her
Yaffa, the Hebrew word for "pretty."

Time passes. Now it is fall. Soon it will be winter. A flock of storks makes its way back to warm Africa. A passing male stork spots Yaffa and flies lower for a closer look. Landing on a pole, he spreads his wings, taps his feet, and fans his tail, trying to convince her to join him.

Maya watches. She takes out her walkie-talkie. "Come quick," she calls to her abba.

Her father looks at the bird. "He'll give up and fly away."

But the stork does not give up. He starts building a nest high up on a nearby tree.

"Yaffa can't get up there," says Maya.

"Let's build a nest big enough for two, and maybe he'll come down," her father said.

But the plan does not work. The male stork won't fly down. He continues to expand his own nest. Maya names him Tzadok, the Hebrew word for "righteous."

Months pass. The seasons change. Now it is spring, and storks are once again leaving Africa for a cooler climate. One female sees Tzadok in his nest and flies in for a landing.

"Uh-oh," says Maya.

A month later three little chicks are born. The new mama stands guard over her babies.

Tzadok is a good father. He scavenges for food, proudly bringing home worms, bugs, and frogs. The baby storks happily clack their bills. Down below, Maya, Abba, and Yaffa watch the family grow.

When the babies reach two months, Mama stork stands straight, flaps her wings, and flies off.

"What's going on?" asks Maya.

"The chicks are old enough to fly," Abba says. "Mama is getting ready to teach them how, but first she has to find a practice route."

When night falls, Mama stork is not back. The chicks begin to whimper. A week goes by. Still no Mama.

The chicks are hungry and Tzadok cannot leave them to forage for food. He flaps his wings. The flapping gets louder, and louder, **and louder**.

"Poor Tzadok," sighs Abba. "He's worried the chicks will starve."

"Where has the mama gone?" asks Maya.

"Who knows?" answers Abba. "There are so many dangers out there. Remember what happened to Yaffa."

"How can we help?" she asks.

Abba scratches his head and thinks. Then he smiles and whispers his plan to Maya.

"Perfect!" she grins, giving him a hug.

Abba calls to one of the farmers, then starts the engine of a bucket loader.

Maya climbs inside the bucket. The farmer carefully places Yaffa in her arms, then hops up beside her.

"Higher!" cries Maya until the bucket reaches the nest. Tzadok quickly opens and closes his beak, making a noisy, clattering sound. The babies begin to chirp.

When they reach the nest, the farmer gently strokes Tzadok and the babies. "Everything will be all right," he assures them.

"Easy does it," says Maya, carefully placing Yaffa in the nest. The frightened chicks snuggle closer to Tzadok. He spreads his wings over them and Yaffa.

"Finally," whispers Maya to herself. "Mission accomplished, Abba," she radios, as she waves to the new family of storks.

Born in the United States, Tami Lehman-Wilzig now lives in Israel. She has a Bachelor's Degree in English Literature and a Master's Degree in Communications from Boston University. She is one of Israel's leading English language copywriters. Her children's books include *Tasty Bible Stories*, *Keeping the Promise*, *Passover Around the World*, *Hanukkah Around the World*, *Zvuvi's Israel*, and *Nathan Blows Out the Hanukkah Candles*. She lives in Petach Tikvah.

Anna Shuttlewood has a Bachelor's Degree in Mural Painting and Fine Arts from the National Academy of Arts in Sofia, Bulgaria. Her murals can be seen at various sites across Europe, including the National Library in Sofia, the Royal United Hospital in Bath, and the Bloom Hotel in Brussels. She also produces smaller scale compositions using both classical and contemporary techniques, and has illustrated many children's books.